ALLAN FREWIN JONES

Anna's Birthday Adventure

Illustrated by Judy Brown

MACDONALD YOUNG BOOKS

1124018

Chapter One

It was Anna's birthday. At last! She woke up feeling very, very excited. She ran down the stairs two at a time.

"Happy Birthday!" said Mum and Dad together.

"Hooray!" shouted Anna as she saw the pile of presents on the living-room floor. She had some really wonderful presents. She was still ripping wrapping paper and tearing tissue when Granny arrived on her motor bike and gave Anna yet another present.

What a brilliant birthday!

Suddenly Anna realized something.

"Where is Uncle Oscar's present?" she asked. "Uncle Oscar promised to send me a very special present this year."

Anna had never met her Uncle Oscar.

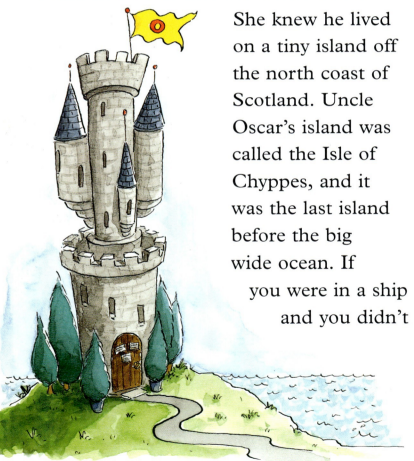

She knew he lived on a tiny island off the north coast of Scotland. Uncle Oscar's island was called the Isle of Chyppes, and it was the last island before the big wide ocean. If you were in a ship and you didn't stop at the Isle of Chyppes, you wouldn't see dry land again for six whole weeks.

Uncle Oscar had spent years travelling all over the world, exploring sweltering jungles and climbing gigantic mountains and diving into great big rivers and being lowered on ropes into deep, dark caves. He was

enormously rich and had retired to a tall stone tower on the Isle of Chyppes to write his life story.

A few weeks ago Uncle Oscar had written a letter to Anna.

The letter said this:

Dear Anna

I am very sorry that I have been too busy exploring to have ever met you. I would like to make up for this by buying you a very special birthday present on your next birthday. I am afraid I don't know what girls like for birthday presents. Please write to me with a list of the sort of presents you would like.

Yours truly

Uncle Oscar

Anna had written a letter to Uncle Oscar, thanking him for thinking of her (this was her mum's idea) and enclosing a list of things she would like for her birthday (these were all Anna's ideas).

And now the morning of her birthday had arrived. But a special birthday parcel from Uncle Oscar definitely hadn't arrived!

"Perhaps he forgot," said Anna's mum. "You must remember that your Uncle Oscar is a very unusual man. And unusual men sometimes forget things that ordinary people remember. I'm sure he didn't mean to upset you."

"I'm not upset," said Anna trying her
best not to look upset.

Chapter Two

Mum and Dad had to go and do some shopping. Granny stayed with Anna and showed her how to make an armchair into a perfect tent by tipping it over on to its side and hanging a table cloth over it.

Anna and her granny sat in their tent and watched television through a small gap in the table cloth.

"It's much more fun watching television like this," Granny said. "I don't know why more people don't do it." Granny smiled at

Anna. "Are you having a nice birthday?"
she asked.

Anna nodded. "Yes," she said. "It's very
nice. But I still wish Uncle Oscar's present
had arrived. Do you think he forgot all
about me?"

"I don't know," said Granny. "But there's
one way to find out."

"We could telephone him!" said Anna.

"He doesn't have a telephone," said
Granny. "But if you asked me, I'd say that
the best way of finding out what happened
to your birthday present would be to go up

to your Uncle Oscar's house, knock on the
door and say 'Hello, Uncle Oscar, how do
you do? I'm your niece Anna and it's my
birthday today in case you *forgot*.' "

"But it's such a long way," sighed Anna.
"How would I *ever* get there?"

"I could take you on my motor bike,"
said Granny.

"Wow!" said Anna, and the next thing
she knew she was sitting behind her granny
on the great big motor bike, wearing a
helmet that nearly covered her eyes while
they zoomed along the
road at a great speed.

Anna had written her mum and dad a quick note to explain where she was going, so they wouldn't worry about her.

The motor bike gobbled up the miles and they soon left the town behind. Granny sang sea-shanties and pirate songs as they whooshed along. At this speed they would get to Uncle Oscar's island in no time!

Crunch! Grinch! Grunch! Gronch! Ptoing! Put-put-bleeergh! Sploooooooop!

"Oh dear," said Granny as the motor bike came to a grinding halt at the roadside. "Something is very wrong. Oh, pooh! Now what shall we do?"

Chapter Three

They both climbed off the motor bike.
Anna sat on a grassy slope while Granny
muttered at the motor bike and hit it here
and there with a large spanner.

"Do you know what's wrong?" asked
Anna.

"Yes," said Granny. "The twinge-flange is
broken. It's a very simple repair. All it
needs is a new twinge-flange." Granny
sighed. "I haven't got a new twinge-flange."

"Oh, dear," said Anna. Then she said. "Hello, what's this?" as a dark, round shadow came creeping across the grass.

They both looked up. It was a huge red hot-air balloon.

"Hello down there," called a woman wearing a flying-helmet and goggles. "Lovely day for it." And she waved cheerfully.

"Excuse me," Anna called, "do you have a spare twinge-flange you could lend us?"

"I'm afraid not," said the balloonist. "But you're very welcome to come aboard. I'll take you to the nearest town. I'm sure someone there will have what you need."

A rope ladder came spinning down from the balloon's wicker basket. Anna and her granny climbed up and the balloonist rolled the ladder back up again.

The balloonist pulled a lever and a propeller began to turn. Anna leaned over the edge of the basket. Her granny's motor bike already looked like a toy. Soon it was

just a tiny dot as the
balloon chugged along
over open countryside.

"Care for a
sandwich?" asked the balloonist opening a
large wicker hamper. Anna and her granny
and the balloonist all sat down to eat.

Suddenly there was a terrible roaring
noise.

Rooaaarrrrrr. Whooooooooosh.

Something long and thin and silver-
coloured burst right through the balloon
with a huge *BANG!*

Anna and her granny clung on for dear
life as the basket rocked and the balloon
sagged and hissed.

The balloonist looked over the side.
"Bangers and mash!" she said. "We're
going to crash!"

But they didn't crash. They came down
very softly, as though they had landed in a
giant heap of feathers.

Chapter Four

A few seconds later an anxious face peered over the side of the basket.

"I'm terribly sorry," said the bald-headed man, looking worriedly at the three people in the basket. "You got in the way of an experiment of mine."

He helped them out of the basket. Nearby was a small concrete bunker with a long metal tube sticking out of the roof.

Anna climbed out of the basket and fell waist-deep into feathers.

"I'm experimenting with rockets," said the man, helping Anna to her feet. "These feathers are to save the rockets from getting bent when they crash." He sighed. "They nearly all crash," he said. "You see, the problem is that they really need pilots." He pointed to himself. "I can't pilot them because I have to press the button that fires them." He blinked at Anna and her Granny.

"I don't suppose either of you know how to pilot a rocket?" he asked hopefully.

"I'm a quick learner," said Anna helpfully.

"I'm off," said the balloonist. "I can't stand rockets!"

The bald-headed man led Anna and her granny to his bunker. "It's really very simple," he said as he strapped Anna into a seat in the nose-cone of the rocket. He showed her the controls while her granny squeezed into the co-pilot's seat.

The man closed the nose-cone door. Over the intercom Anna heard:

"Fivefourthreetwoone! Blast off!"

Anna was pressed back in her seat as the rocket shot into the air.

They burst through a cloud and came out into brilliant sunshine. Anna waved at a very surprised-looking bird. For a while all they could see was the blue sky. Then the blueness got darker. Then it got darker still. And all of a sudden it was quite black and the whole sky was full of stars.

"It's night-time!" said Anna.

"No, it's not," said her granny. "We're in outer space!"

A roly-poly satellite cartwheeled by, making a beeping noise. The rocket shot twice around the satellite and then headed downwards.

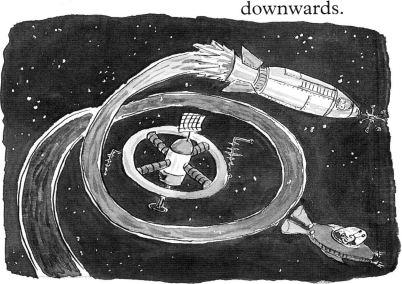

"Wheeeee!" shouted Anna as the sky turned blue again. A few moments later she could see the whole of the country spread out like a weather map, green and friendly in the blue of the sea.

The land got bigger and bigger, and the rocket went faster and faster. Suddenly all Anna could see was mountains rushing up towards the rocket.

"Oh! Help!" said Anna as an especially tall peak came galloping towards them.

There was a gentle bump, a slide and a slither and a *whumph*! as the rocket came to a halt on the highest slopes of the snowy mountainside.

Chapter Five

A red light winked on and off in front of Anna.

"Open in case of emergency," Anna read. She opened the drawer and pulled out two pairs of rollerblades.

"How very useful," said her granny as the two of them climbed out of the rocket. The snow was only a little cap on the top of the mountain. They walked down to where the snow ended and put on their rollerblades.

"Now then," said Anna. "We will probably go very fast, so we should hold hands."

Anna took a tight hold of her granny's hand.

"One, two, three, GO!"

Vwoooooooooooooom!

Hand in hand they shot down the mountainside like pellets from a catapult. Every now and then Anna had to adjust her balance so she didn't fall over. She found out that she was very good at rollerblading.

They came to a deep valley and before they knew it they had crossed the bottom and were whipping up the other side and over a sharp edge. For a few seconds they hung in mid air before they landed again and whooshed down the next slope.

Anna got used to it. Whoosh down into a valley. Wheee! up the next slope! Yee-haaah! as they flew into the air and Thumpetty! as they landed on the next bit of mountain.

Wheee!

Yee-haaah!

"Oops!" said Anna.

SPLASHAROONIE!

The mountains had ended.
Anna and her granny had flown over the
last ridge and splooshed straight into water.

Anna spluttered. It was salt water. They
were in the sea. Anna was just trying to
remember how to swim when something
long and rounded and sleek came up under
her and she found herself sitting astride a
dolphin.

She wiped the water out of her eyes and saw that her granny was sitting on an even bigger dolphin.

"That was a bit of luck!" said Granny with a grin.

Before Anna could think of a reply, the two dolphins began swimming at a great speed out into the open sea.

"Hey!" said Anna, tapping gently on her dolphin's head. She pointed back to the land. "We want to go that way!"

"Chik! Chik! Chik! Chi-h-ih-ih-ik," said the dolphin.

"Granny," Anna called. "Do you speak dolphin?"

"I'm afraid not," said her granny. "I think we'll just have to trust them to take us somewhere safe."

It wasn't long before the land dropped below the horizon and they were out in the empty sea.

Where on earth were the dolphins going?

Suddenly Anna noticed a shoal of flying fish all dipping in and out of the water together. As the shoal came closer Anna could hear tiny high-pitched voices all singing in chorus.

She stared in amazement as the cloud of leaping fish got closer and closer until she could hear exactly what they were singing.

"Happy birthday to you, happy birthday to you, happy birthday dear Anna, happy birthday to you!" they sang. And then there was a burst of cheering and laughter as the shoal of fish dived one last time back into the water and disappeared.

Chapter Six

"This is very odd," thought Anna. "How did they know it was my birthday?"

"Land ho!" called Anna's granny. Anna looked over to where she was pointing. It was funny-looking land, she thought. It was perfectly flat and very small.

As they got closer, Anna could see that it was a wooden raft. On the raft sat a woman in a deck-chair reading a newspaper.

"Hello Polly!" said the woman, jumping up. "Hello Dolly!"

"Er, my name's Anna," said Anna. "Not Polly or Dolly. And this is my granny."

The woman grinned the toothiest grin that Anna had ever seen. "I was saying hello to my two dolphin friends here," she said as she helped Anna and her granny on to the raft. "Are you lost? We don't get many visitors up here."

"We're looking for the Isle of Chyppes," said Anna.

"Well, well," said the raft woman. "I think I can help you." She led Anna and her granny to the far side of the raft, where a tiny motor boat was moored, bobbing in the choppy water.

"I'm afraid there isn't room for both of you on board," said the raft woman. "Would one of you mind water-skiing along behind?"

Anna volunteered to water-ski. Her granny and the raft woman climbed into the tiny boat and the motor started.

"Hold on tight," said the raft woman, "And remember – keep your knees slightly bent and try to *ride* the bigger waves."

The boat shot off. Anna took a firm grip of the rope.

"I hope I can manage this," she said to herself. "I hope I don't – whooooooooooooo-oooooooooooooop!"

For a few moments Anna couldn't tell whether she was on her feet or her elbow or her left ear. Water flooded past her in great white sprays and it felt like her arms were being pulled off.

But then she got her balance and started to enjoy herself. She even tried a few tricks while her granny watched from the back of the boat. Holding on with one hand. Lifting one leg in the air. Lifting the other leg in the air.

She was having a thoroughly good time when the little boat took a sudden turn to the left and Anna lost her grip on the tow-rope.

With a yell, Anna found herself speeding towards a small hump of land with a tall tower in its very middle. Anna waggled her arms and wobbled her legs as she tried to keep upright on the water-skis.

She zoomed up the sandy beach. The skis came to a shuddering halt and Anna was catapulted head over heels into a
thick bush.

She clambered out, plucking bits of twig and leaf out of her hair. She looked back to see where the boat had got to. But of the boat there was not the slightest sign.

Anna walked up the path that led to the lonely tower.

On the huge black wooden door hung a crooked sign.

Oscar's Tower, it said.

"Aha!" said Anna to herself. "I've landed on the Isle of Chyppes! Brilliant!"

No hawkers, said the crooked sign. No circulars, no sellers of double glazing or central heating. No visitors of any sort whatsoever. This means YOU!

"It can't really mean me," Anna thought as she pressed the doorbell under a sign which said: DON'T RING!

Chapter Seven

Anna waited. There was the sound of hollow, echoey footsteps. Anna waited a bit longer. Eventually the huge door creaked slowly open and an impressive moustache appeared somewhere near the top.

"Hello, Uncle Oscar!" exclaimed Anna. "I'm your niece, Anna, and it's my birthday today in case you forgot!"

A pair of twinkly eyes peered down at Anna from above a long lumpy nose.

"I've been expecting you," said Uncle Oscar with a huge beaming smile. "Come on in, my dear, and a happy birthday to you!"

"Excuse me," said Anna as she stepped over the threshold into a long dark corridor. "But you *can't* have been expecting me."

"Oh, but I was," said Uncle Oscar as he led Anna towards a big pair of closed doors. "We *all* were!"

Uncle Oscar opened the doors. Anna was almost bowled over by a huge cheer! The room beyond was decorated for a party. There was a table filled with food and drinks and the room was filled with people.

Anna stood there with her mouth hanging open. Mum and Dad were there. So was Granny. So was the balloonist and the man with the rockets. And so was the

raft woman. As well as all Anna's friends from school and all her other uncles and aunts and cousins.

Uncle Oscar pushed Anna into the party room and everyone started singing "Happy Birthday to You"!

Mum and Dad gave her a big hug. "Surprise!"

"But … but …" said Anna. "But I thought Uncle Oscar had forgotten!"

"Not a bit of it," said Uncle Oscar. He pulled a piece of paper out of his pocket. "Now then," he said. "Let's see if I remembered everything."

Anna recognized the sheet of paper. It was the list of birthday presents she had sent to Uncle Oscar.

Uncle Oscar began to read the list.

"I would like a ride on a motor bike, please!" he read. "Or I would like to have a go in a hot-air balloon. Or I would like to see how a rocket works." Uncle Oscar ticked each request off with a red pen. "Yes, yes, yes," he said.

Then he carried on reading. "I would like a pair of rollerblades," he read. "I would like to meet a dolphin. I would also like to learn to water-ski. And most of all, I would like a big party."

Uncle Oscar ticked away with his red pen. "Yes, yes, yes," he said. "And finally: YES!"

And everyone laughed and cheered as Anna was led to the seat of honour at the end of the table.

"And I thought you'd forgotten!" she said with the biggest smile she had ever smiled.

It was the best birthday present Anna had ever been given. And to top it all, everyone was taken home afterwards by submarine. As Anna told her mum as she snuggled happily into bed that night, a ride in a submarine was something she had *thought* of putting on the birthday present list, but she had left it off because she didn't want Uncle Oscar to think she was being greedy.

Look out for more exciting titles in the yellow Storybook series:

Sir Garibald and Hot Nose by Marjorie Newman
Sir Garibald lives with his dragon, Hot Nose, in their dark, creepy castle with no electricity. What they need is a large sum of money. So they devise a cunning, but not quite honest, scheme that doesn't quite go to plan…

Emily's Legs by Dick King-Smith
At first, nobody noticed Emily's legs. Then, at the Spider Sports, everyone began to ask questions.

I Want That Pony! by Christine Pullein-Thompson
Sophy is desperate to own Flash, the pony that lives down the lane. But Flash already has an owner, who doesn't want to give him up.

Maxie's Music by Elizabeth Dale
Maxie loves playing music, and the louder the better. But her family doesn't appreciate her talent. Not until one very exciting night when Maxie's musical gift makes her a hero.

Gilly the Kid by Adèle Geras
Gilly the Kid is a cowgirl. She can round up cattle, throw a lasso and ride faster than anyone south-west of Coyote Canyon. But what she'd like to do is catch some real live baddies.

All these books and many more in the Storybook series can be purchased from your local bookseller. For more information about Storybooks, write to: *The Sales Department, Macdonald Young Books, 61 Western Road, Hove, East Sussex BN3 1JD.*